This book belongs to

....

This is a story about Snow White,

You can read it by day or read it at night!

There's something else. Can you guess what?

Throughout this book there's a robin to spot.

Snow White

Nick and Claire Page

Illustrations by Bee Willey

make
believe
ideas

Once there was a young princess with skin as white as snow, lips as red as blood and hair as black as ebony. She was called Snow White.

Her mother was dead and her father
had married again. The new queen was
beautiful but vain. Every day she asked:
"Mirror, mirror on the wall,
Who is the fairest of them all?"
And the mirror replied:
"You, O Queen, are the fairest, it's true,
No one else is a looker like you."

As each year passed, Snow White grew
more beautiful. One day, the queen said
to her mirror:

**"Mirror, mirror on the wall,
Who is the fairest of them all?"**

The mirror answered:
"You, O Queen, are a lovely sight,
But if you force me to choose,
I'll go for Snow White."
The queen turned yellow with shock,
then green with envy.

So she ordered a huntsman to take Snow
White into the forest and kill her. But the
huntsman felt sorry for Snow White and let
her go. She ran through the forest, until she
came to a tiny house.

Inside, there was a table with seven places and seven little beds. Snow White lay on the beds and fell asleep.

Later, seven dwarfs came home from digging in the mines. They were surprised to find Snow White in their home!

"Who are you?" she asked.
"We are Monday, Tuesday, Wednesday,
Thursday, Friday, Saturday and Fred,"
they said.

The dwarfs agreed to let Snow White
stay to look after the house and cook
their meals.

Back at the palace, the queen asked again:
"Mirror, mirror on the wall,
Who is the fairest of them all?"

And the mirror replied:
"You, O Queen, have the beauty of night,
But you're still coming second to
Princess Snow White.
She's still alive and still good-looking,
She lives with the dwarfs and does
their cooking."

The Queen turned purple with passion and red with rage.

So, using her magic, she went to the
cottage disguised as an old woman:
"Try my apples. Take a bite!
Just the thing for skin so white!"

Snow White didn't know it was the queen, so she bought a juicy red apple. But the apple was poisoned and when Snow White took a bite she fell down, as if dead.

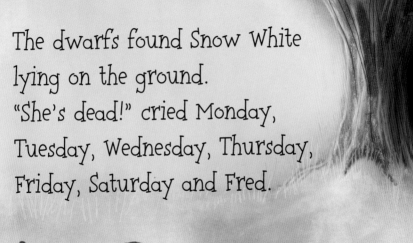

The dwarfs found Snow White
lying on the ground.
"She's dead!" cried Monday,
Tuesday, Wednesday, Thursday,
Friday, Saturday and Fred.

They put her in a glass coffin
and took turns to guard it.

The queen ran back to the palace.
**"Mirror, mirror on the wall,
Who is the fairest of them all?"**

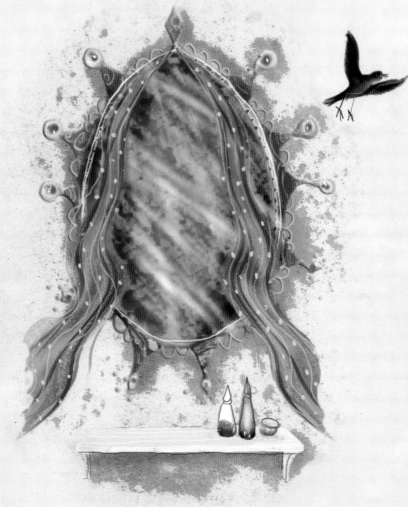

And the mirror replied, sadly:
"You, O Queen, are the fairest of fair.
Snow White's dead, so what do I care?"

One day, a prince came riding through the forest and saw Snow White lying there, her skin as white as snow, lips as red as blood and hair as black as ebony.

At once he fell in love. "Let me take her back to my castle," he begged. "I cannot live without her."

As his servants lifted the coffin, one
tripped and the piece of poisoned apple
fell out of Snow White's mouth.

At once Snow White woke up!
"She's not dead!" cried Monday, Tuesday,
Wednesday, Thursday, Friday, Saturday
and Fred.

Back at the castle, as usual, the
queen asked her mirror:
"Mirror, mirror on the wall,
Who is the fairest of them all?"
And the mirror answered:
"You, O Queen, are far from plain,
But Snow White is alive again!"

At this, the queen turned every color
under the sun, all at once, until she
shattered into a thousand pieces.

So Snow White married the prince. And the seven dwarfs came and saw them every day: Monday, Tuesday, Wednesday, Thursday, Friday, Saturday and Fred.

Ready to tell

Oh no! Some of the pictures from this story have been mixed up! Can you retell the story and point to each picture in the correct order?

Picture dictionary

Encourage your child to read these harder
words from the story and gradually develop
their basic vocabulary.

beautiful

disguised

dwarf

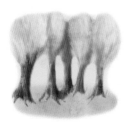

forest

mirror

palace

prince

princess

shattered

Key words

Here are some key words used in context.
Help your child to use other words from
the border in simple sentences.

Snow White **was** beautiful.

The queen did not **like** her.

The mirror **said**...

The prince saw Snow White.

They were happy.

Make a magic mirror

You may not be able to make a truly magic mirror, but it's easy to make a mirror that's fit for a princess.

You will need

a mirror tile • sticky tape • a large sheet of cardboard
• a pencil • a ruler • paint or crayons • glue
• beads, feathers, toy jewels and pieces of tissue paper

What to do

1 Take care! Some tiles have sharp edges. Ask a grown-up to put tape around the edges to make them safe.
2 Carefully lay the tile on the middle of the cardboard and draw around it.
3 Ask a grown-up to draw one line about an inch outside the square you have drawn, and another ½ inch inside.
4 Cut along the two new lines to make a simple frame. (You may need a grown-up to help you.)

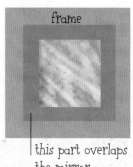

frame

this part overlaps the mirror

5 Color the cardboard, using crayons or paint (let it dry). Glue beads, jewels, feathers, or bits of tissue paper on one side of the frame. Make it look really special.
6 When the glue has dried, carefully stick the tile to the other side using strong tape.
Turn it over and you have a "magic" mirror of your own!